Disney · PIXAR

MONSTERS UNIVERSITY

GIVE US A ROAR!

Adapted by Cynthia Hands
Illustrated by the Disney Storybook Artists

A GOLDEN BOOK • NEW YORK

ISBN 978-0-7364-3040-1
randomhouse.com/kids
Printed in the United States of America
10 9 8 7 6 5 4 3 2 1

It's a big day for young Mike Wazowski.
He's going on a field trip to Monsters, Inc.

Monsters called Scarers collect scream energy
from the human world.

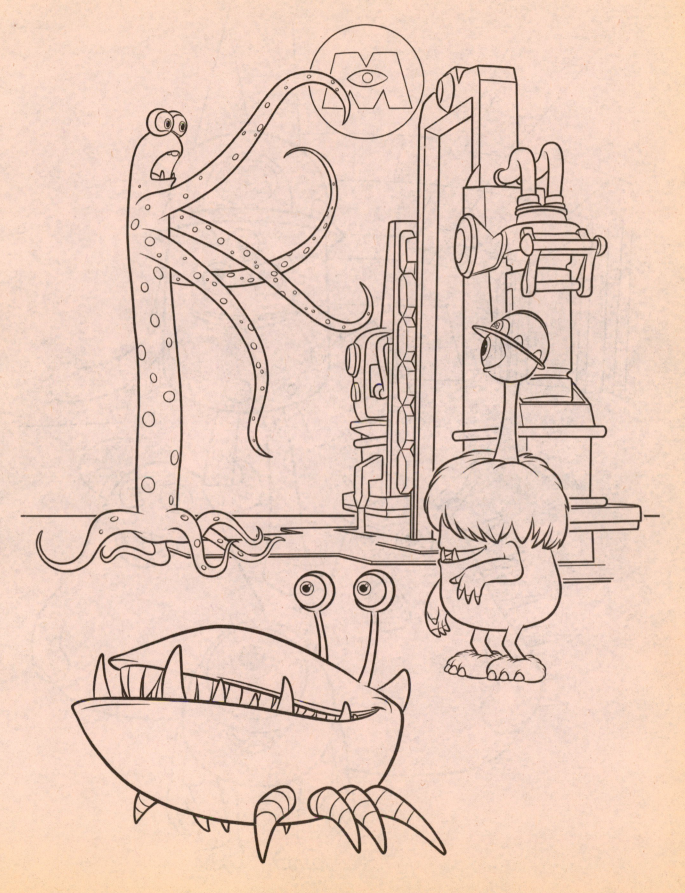

Mike enjoys the tour of the scare floor. He learns a lot about scream energy and what it takes to be a Scarer.

Mike wants to learn more, so he sneaks into the human world to watch a real Scarer at work.

"Frightening" Frank McCay tells Mike that the best place to learn
how to be a Scarer is Monsters University.
Use the key below to color Mike and Frightening Frank.

COLOR KEY
1 = Green
2 = Light Blue
3 = Medium Blue
4 = Dark Blue
5 = Yellow

Mike grows up and goes to school at Monsters University. His plan is to become the greatest Scarer ever!

Mike gets his Monsters University ID card.
Use your imagination to make your own ID card.

MONSTERS
UNIVERSITY

VALID FALL/SPRING SEMESTER

M.Wazowski

STUDENT

Scaring

MAJOR

Mike Wazowski

SIGNATURE

ID.NO. 600962011054255

MONSTERS
UNIVERSITY

VALID FALL/SPRING SEMESTER

STUDENT

MAJOR

ID.NO. 600962011054255

SIGNATURE

Mike meets his roommate, a monster named Randy Boggs.

Draw lines from each monster to their two close-ups.

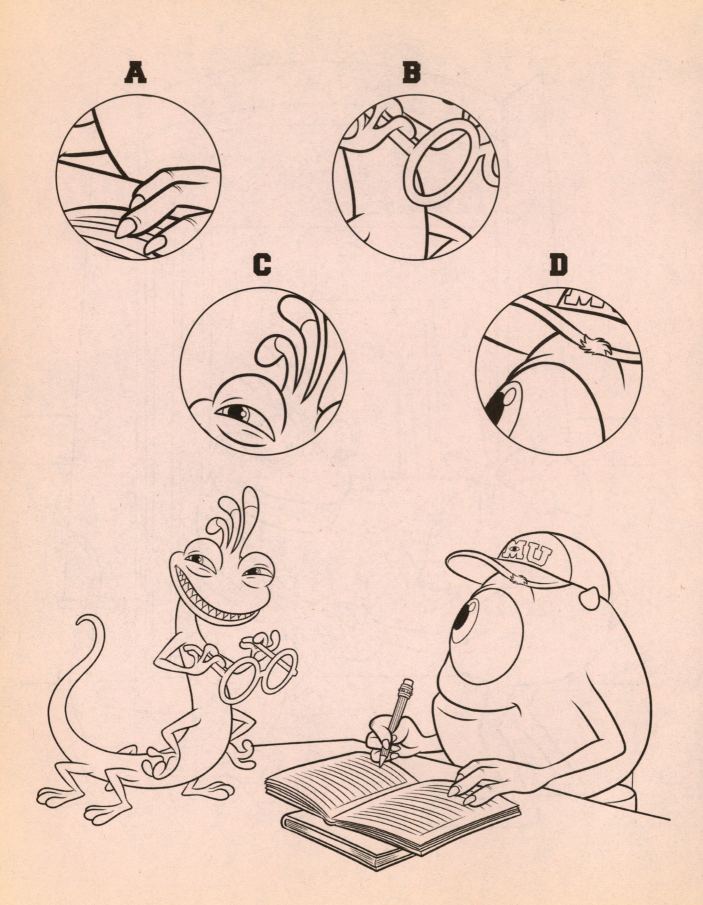

Mike can't wait to get started at the Monsters University
School of Scaring.

Randy and Mike touch the statue before entering the
School of Scaring—it's a tradition.

Professor Knight teaches Scaring 101. All monsters must pass his class if they want to stay in the School of Scaring.

Mike knows all the answers to the scaring questions.

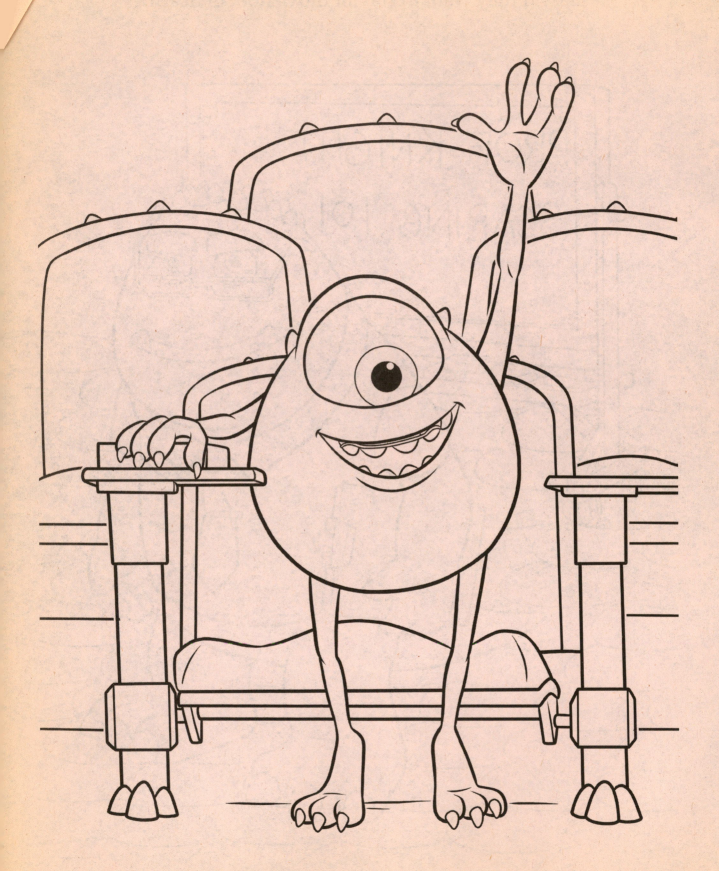

Dean Hardscrabble holds the all-time scare record!
Find and circle the scream can that matches Dean Hardscrabble's legendary canister.

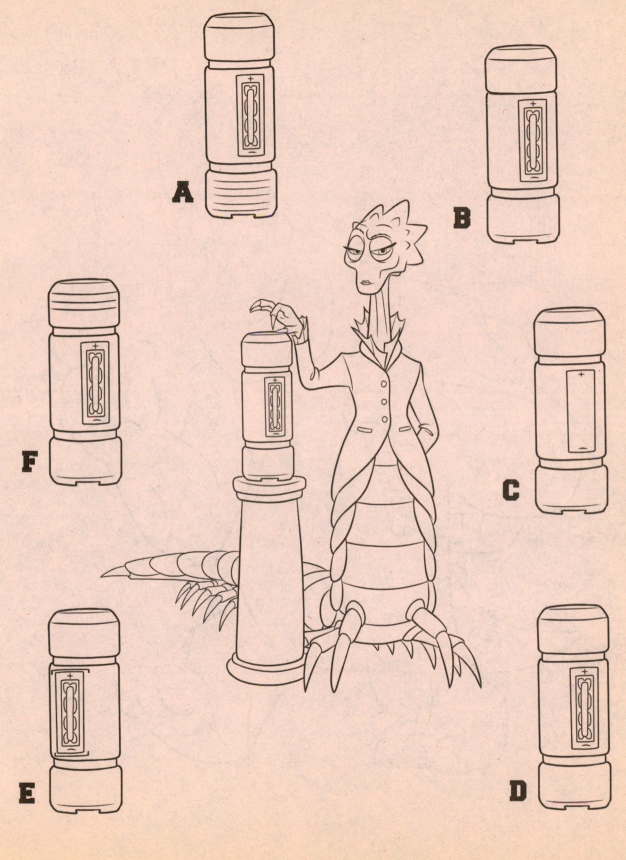

A

B

F

C

E

D

James P. Sullivan is another student in the Scaring Program.
Everyone calls him Sulley.

Randy makes cupcakes to take to a big party!

Archie the Scare Pig is on the loose!

Help Sulley find the path that leads to Mike and Archie. Watch out for Professor Knight and Dean Hardscrabble!

ANSWER: Path 3.

Sulley and Mike celebrate after catching Archie.

Mike works hard to impress Professor Knight.

Sulley just wants to eat and have fun!

Mike doesn't have time for fun—there are too many
books to read!

Sulley isn't interested in books, but he does like to play Ping-Pong.
Help Sulley count and circle the balls in the picture.

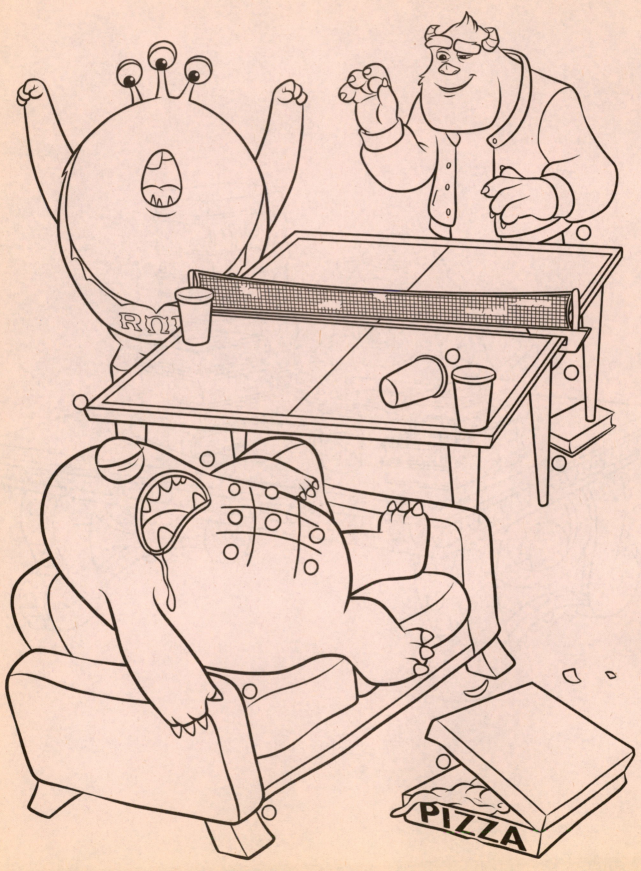

Mike studies everywhere—even at the big football game!

Sulley meets Johnny, the leader of the ROR team.

Use the code to find out more about Johnny.

Σ	Ᵹ	Φ	Λ	Ψ	Π	Γ	Ⴈ	M	Ⴑ	Ⴈ	Ⴅ	⊕	Ᵹ
A	**B**	**C**	**D**	**E**	**G**	**H**	**I**	**M**	**N**	**R**	**S**	**T**	**Y**

Mike tries to outrun Sulley.

The big test is about to begin! Mike and Sulley practice roaring, but
they get a little out of hand!

Sulley and Mike get kicked out of the Scaring Program after they break Dean Hardscrabble's prized scream can!

Mike and Sulley take a Scream Can Design class. Use your imagination to design and color your own scream can.

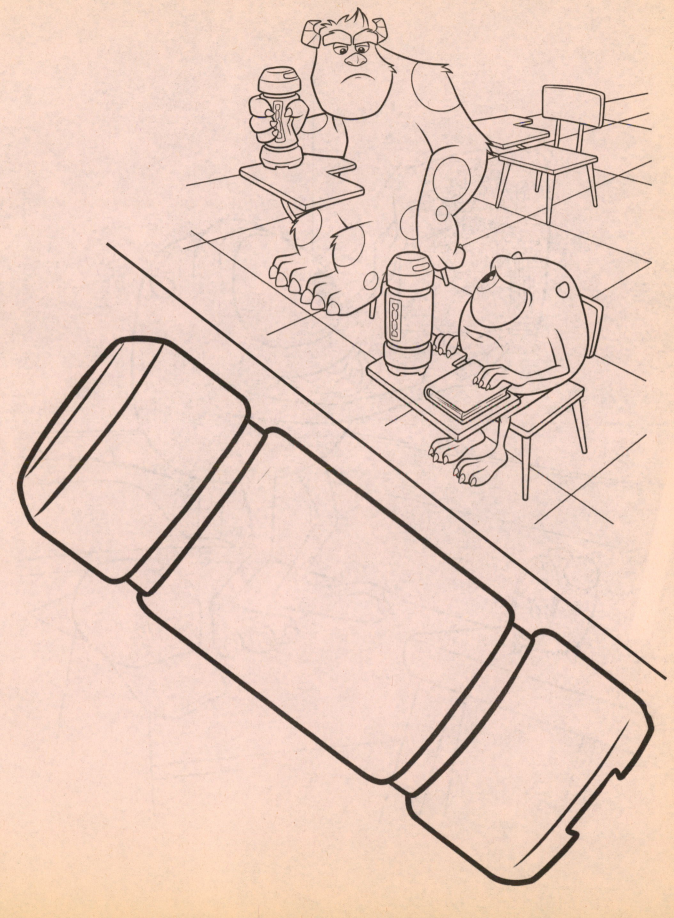

Mike wants to compete in the Scare Games so he can get back into the Scaring Program.

Mike and Sulley join the Oozma Kappa team to get into the
Scare Games.

Unfortunately, the Oozma Kappa monsters are too nice
to be scary.

Don is the president of OK.

The OKs try to have a party to welcome Mike and Sulley.

Terri and Terry are brothers—who share the same body! Circle the
picture of Terri and Terry that is different from the others.

Art is mysterious . . . and a little weird!

Sulley doesn't believe Mike can teach the OKs how to be scary.

Squishy is a sweet little monster. He welcomes all new OK members.

Ms. Squibbles is Squishy's mother. The OKs live in her house.

Don, Terri, and Terry take the welcoming of new members very seriously.

Ms. Squibbles is Squishy's mother. The OKs live in her house.

Don, Terri, and Terry take the welcoming of new members
very seriously.

Mike and Sulley have to share a room, but they don't get along very well—except when they're sleeping.

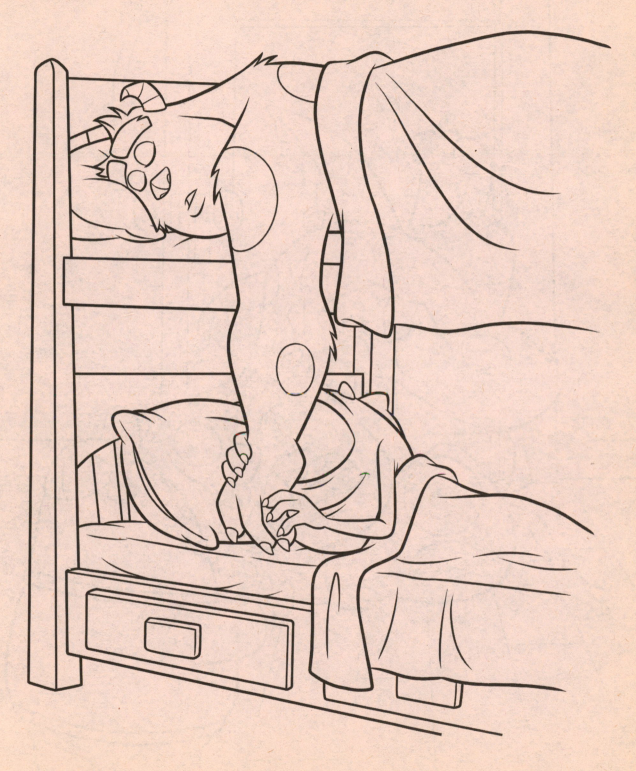

Squishy takes a picture of Mike and Sulley when they get stuck in the door.

The OK team competes against the ROR team in the Scare Games.

ROAR OMEGA ROAR

Jaws Theta Chi is also taking part in the Scare Games.

JAWS THETA CHI

Slugma Slugma Kappa is known as EEK.

SLUGMA SLUGMA KAPPA

The PNKs always wear pink.

PYTHON NU KAPPA

Slugma Slugma Kappa is known as EEK.

SLUGMA SLUGMA KAPPA

The PNKs always wear pink.

PYTHON NU KAPPA

The HSS team is the final team competing in the Scare Games.

ETA HISS HISS

In the first event of the Scare Games, the monsters must run through a tunnel filled with stinging glow urchins!

Art thinks touching a stinging glow urchin will be fun, but it's not!

Mike and Sulley lead the OKs through the tunnel, but the team is in last place!

The JOX cheated and got kicked out of the Scare Games!
The OKs move on to the next event.

How many times can you find JOX in the puzzle? Look up, down,
forward, backward, and diagonally.

O	J	J	O
J	O	X	X
X	X	O	J
O	J	J	O

In the second event, the monsters have to sneak around the watchful librarian and get their team flag.

Sulley made too much noise, and now the librarian is after him!

Squishy is awesome! He grabs the OK flag and wins the event!

ROAR OMEGA ROAR WORD FIND

Look up, down, forward, backward, and diagonally
to find all the names.

☐ CHET

☐ JOHNNY

☐ RANDY

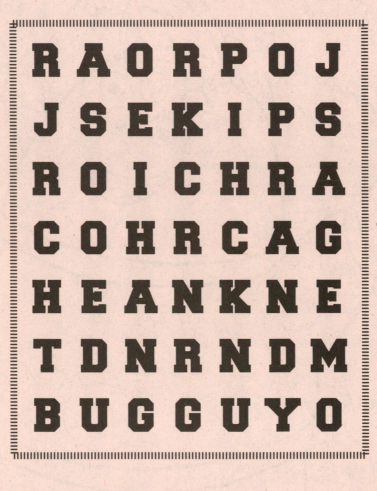

R A O R P O J
J S E K I P S
R O I C H R A
C O H R C A G
H E A N K N E
T D N R N D M
B U G G U Y O

☐ SPIKES

☐ BUGGUY

ANSWER:

Mike and the OKs visit Monsters, Inc., to watch Scarers at work.
They learn that it's good to be different.

The OKs make a quick escape when a guard spots them
on the roof of Monsters, Inc.

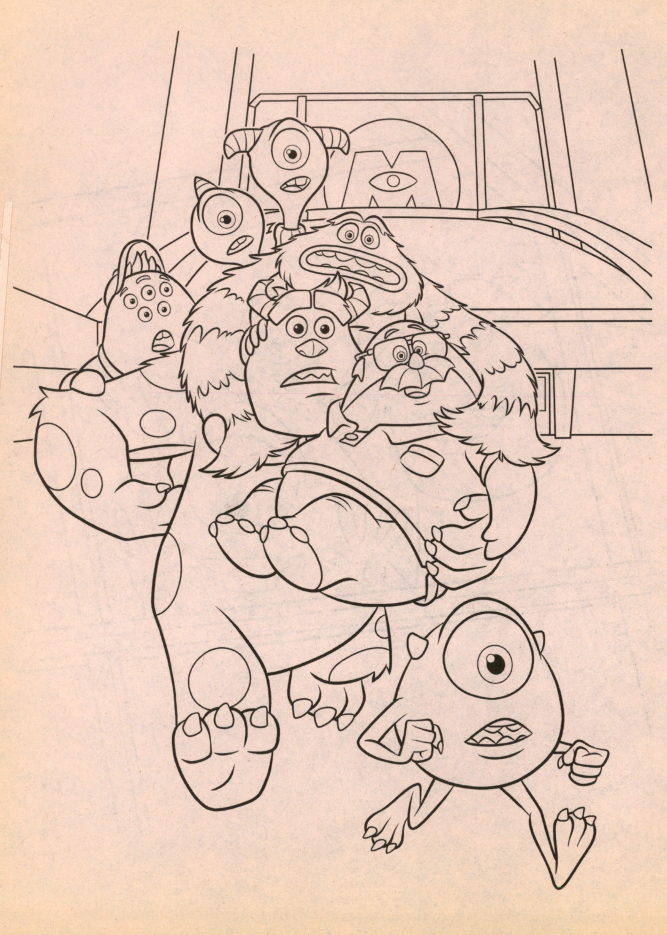

Mike really knows how to bring out the best in the OKs—
he's a great coach!

The team gets better when Sulley starts to take training seriously.

Squishy trains hard for the Scare Games.

Art and Squishy do a good job in the Scare the Teen event.

The third event in the Scare Games is a maze.
Help Squishy and Art find Mike.

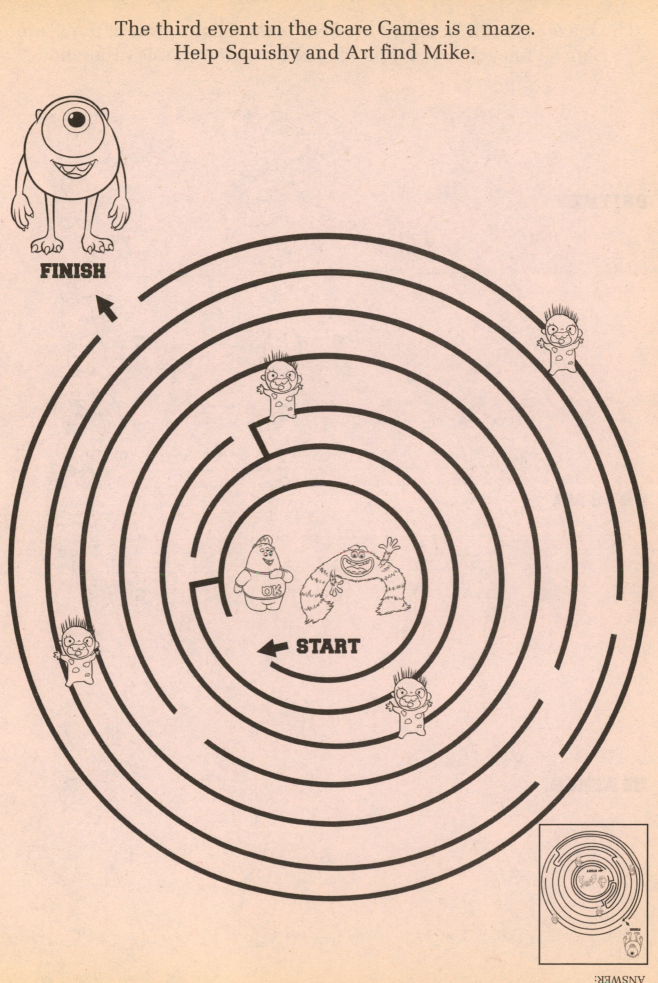

FINISH

START

ANSWER:

The maze is too difficult for the PNK team. They're out of the Scare Games! In each row, circle the PNK monster that is different.

BRITNEY

A   B   C

CRYSTAL

A   B   C

HEATHER

A   B   C

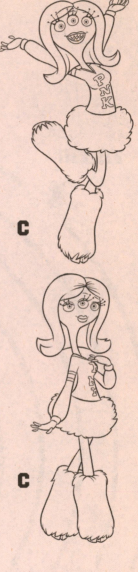

Squishy trains hard for the Scare Games.

Art and Squishy do a good job in the Scare the Teen event.

Mike teaches Don how to use the suction cups on his tentacles while the other OKs practice their talents.

In the fourth event, the referees have to find the hiding monsters.

Mike is proud when Don uses his tentacles to stick to
the ceiling and avoid a referee.

The HSS team lose, so they are out of the Scare Games.
Look at the top picture carefully. Then circle five things that
are different in the bottom picture.

ANSWER:

Sulley thinks Mike is the heart and soul of the OK team, but Dean Hardscrabble doesn't believe Mike will ever be a good Scarer.

Sulley shares a few scaring tips with Mike.

It's time for the OKs' biggest challenge—the last scaring game against the ROR team!

During the fifth and final event, Mike *ROARS* louder than he ever has before!

Mike is amazed that his roar fills a scream can to the top!

Mike is a hero! The OKs defeat the RORs and win the
Scare Games!

Mike finds out the truth—Sulley cheated! He made it easy for Mike to win.

The RORs want Sulley to join them, but Sulley wants to stay with the OKs.

Dean Hardscrabble isn't surprised when Sulley
admits that he cheated.

Mike wants to prove to everyone that he is a good Scarer.
He sneaks into the human world to scare a real child!

In the human world, Mike puts everything he's learned
into one big scare!

Mike roars, but the children laugh. Mike finally realizes that he's just not very scary.

Sulley finds out that Mike went into the human world.

Don helps Sulley get through a door to the human world.

Help Sulley follow the right path so he can save Mike.
Watch out for the rangers!

FINISH

1

2

3

FINISH

ANSWER: Path 2.

Sulley finds Mike, who is sad about not being scary.

Mike and Sulley get chased by the rangers!

Sulley and Mike are trapped! They need to create
a big scare to power up the door!

Mike and Sulley make a great scare team! They fill enough scare cans to return to the monster world.

As soon as they return, Mike and Sulley are in big trouble.

The OKs are accepted into the Scaring Program, but Mike and Sulley are thrown out of Monsters University.

Dean Hardscrabble gives Mike and Sulley a paper. They find
an ad for jobs at Monsters, Inc.

There's a bright future for Wazowski and Sullivan at Monsters, Inc.